MURDER ON THE LAKE

A CELEBRITY DISAPPEARANCE COZY MYSTERY WITH A FAKE DEATH, A PROM QUEEN, AND A KILLER COMEBACK

MONTANA COZY ART MYSTERIES

MOLLIE MATHEWS

Blue Orchid
PUBLISHING

MONTANA COZY ART MYSTERIES

MONTANA COZY ART MYSTERIES

MOLLIE MATHEWS

JOIN THE CLUB

Never miss a new release or giveaway! Sign up for Mollie's newsletter to stay in the loop—and receive a free love story. Check out a full list of books and bio at www.molliemathews.com. Follow Mollie on Social Media as @Molliewritesromance (because she does) And if you loved this book, please take a moment to leave a review once you're done. Thank you!

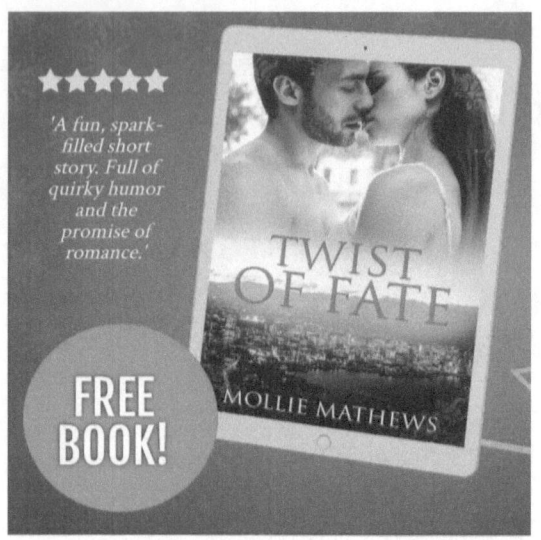

reveal was as satisfying as it was surprising. Highly recommend"

~ Megan W.

ABOUT THIS BOOK

Fame fades. Secrets remain. And in Willow Hollow, even the sweetest melodies can end in murder.

When a country legend's perfect life unravels on the shores of Willow Hollow, secrets rise from the depths...

Everyone at the Willow Hollow Art Retreat is starstruck when Skye Newton, iconic country singer and queen of reinvention, checks in for a private lakeside getaway with her dashing new husband, Troy Landon. But when Troy's shoes are found at the water's edge and he disappears without a trace, the small town is thrown into chaos.

Was it a tragic accident? Or the perfect cover-up?

Cassandra Fairweather suspects the truth is murkier than the lake itself. Rumors fly—of affairs, old flames, and a prom queen with unfinished business. Then, a body washes up... but it's not who anyone expected.

Now, with a scandal ready to explode and a killer lurking close to home, Cassandra must navigate fame, betrayal, and a trail of musical clues to uncover the truth.

Will she solve the mystery before another verse is written in blood?

CHAPTER ONE

Cassandra Fairweather had seen many strange arrivals at Willow Hollow—bohemian painters with too many scarves, burned-out novelists seeking inspiration, and even an alpaca once smuggled in under the guise of a therapy animal.

But nothing—nothing—prepared her for the entrance of Skye Newton, country music legend, draped in denim, diamonds, and scandal.

A hush fell over the retreat as the red vintage Thunderbird eased to a stop outside the main lodge. The door swung open, and out stepped Skye, radiant at sixty, her platinum curls bouncing beneath a wide-brimmed hat, sunglasses too large to be practical, and a leopard-print guitar case slung over one shoulder.

Behind her, a tall, tanned man emerged. He wore a linen shirt unbuttoned just far enough to suggest abs that hadn't come easy and eyes that scanned the scenery like someone more used to yachts than lakeshores.

Troy Landon. Her new husband. Her third, to be precise. Younger by at least fifteen years.

"Cassandra Fairweather?" Skye called in her famous honeyed drawl. "This place is gorgeous. And I've got the paparazzi blocked for seventy-two hours, so let's pretend we're just two regular gals, shall we?"

Cassandra smiled politely. "Welcome to Willow Hollow."

She extended her hand. Skye's fingers were ice-cold and covered in rings.

"I need rest," she said. "And quiet. And maybe just a little revenge songwriting." Her smile didn't quite reach her eyes. "Troy here's been spoiling me rotten, haven't you, sweetheart?"

Troy gave a wink, slung their matching monogrammed bags over one shoulder, and said, "We're hoping this place is private enough for… healing."

Cassandra's smile tightened. She had lived in Willow Hollow long enough to know that when someone asked for privacy, what they really wanted was to escape something.

That evening the lake shimmered under the moonlight. Most of the guests were tucked into bed, bellies full of Susie Sweet's truffle fondue and homemade lavender cider. Cassandra sat alone on the back porch of the lodge, sipping chamomile tea.

Skye had skipped dinner. Said she had a migraine. Troy had gone paddleboarding.

At night.

In the dark.

With a Bluetooth speaker blaring 90s country love ballads.

Cassandra wasn't impressed.

CHAPTER TWO

The fog clung low to the lake, rolling over the still water like silk, soft and silent. Cassandra wrapped her shawl tighter around her shoulders as she stepped onto the porch just after dawn. The scent of pine and last night's rain lingered in the air.

Matisse, her cat, had woken her at five with his usual brand of dramatics—pawing at the bedroom door and howling like a banshee until she relented. Now, with a steaming mug of coffee in hand and the world still hushed with sleep, Cassandra was prepared to enjoy the hush of early morning. The golden light was just beginning to filter through the trees, the lake a perfect mirror.

But something broke the illusion.

A single shape drifted across the water.

A paddleboard.

Alone.

Cassandra squinted and moved to the edge of the dock. The paddleboard glided silently, bumping gently against a boulder on the shoreline. There was no paddle, no rider—just a folded towel and an empty water bottle bobbing in a cupholder.

She descended the wooden stairs and walked toward the rocky beach, her feet crunching softly on the gravel path. Then she saw them—a pair of men's leather boat shoes, placed side by side in the sand.

Neat. Too neat.

Her stomach clenched.

Troy Landon's paddleboard.

Troy Landon's shoes.

But no Troy.

Within the hour, the lodge was buzzing.

Skye Newton was sobbing dramatically on the porch swing, swaddled in a cashmere blanket and clutching a thermos of tea laced—Cassandra suspected—with something stronger. Ruby Thorne tried to soothe her while sneaking worried glances at the lake.

Sheriff Tom Archer stood at the shoreline, arms crossed, watching his deputies search the water with a small rowboat and a drone overhead.

Cassandra stood beside him, hands in her coat pockets.

"You think he fell?" she asked.

Tom shrugged. "Could be. Paddleboarding in the dark is a stupid way to die, but not unheard of."

"No body," Cassandra said.

"Yet."

"No footprints, either," she added. "Shoes placed just so. And the board drifting neatly to the rocks."

Tom grunted. "What are you thinking?"

She hesitated. Then said it aloud.

"I'm thinking he wanted us to believe he drowned."

Tom turned to look at her. "Staged?"

"I'd bet Matisse's whiskers on it."

Tom rubbed the back of his neck. "You think Skye knows?"

Cassandra glanced toward the porch, where Skye now sobbed into a monogrammed handkerchief and muttered lyrics under her breath.

"I think Skye's used to people leaving her," Cassandra said. "But I don't think she expected this one to go without a dramatic goodbye."

Tom exhaled. "Let me guess—you're going to start asking questions."

Cassandra's eyes narrowed as she watched the paddleboard float lazily in the shallows.

"I'm not convinced this is a tragedy," she said quietly. "But I am convinced this is only the beginning."

CHAPTER THREE

By noon, the smell of freshly baked huckleberry scones drifted through the lodge, but no one seemed to notice. Not even Cassandra. The usual calm of Willow Hollow had been pierced by something far more insidious than tragedy—speculation.

"Did you hear?" Ruby whispered, sliding a tray of mugs onto the porch table. "Troy was seen at the Timberline Café. With a blonde."

Cassandra raised an eyebrow. "When?"

"Two days ago. Before Skye even got here. Linda, who works mornings, said they were in a booth by the window— laughing like they were the only two people in the world. And she's sure it wasn't Skye."

"She said it was someone younger?"

Ruby nodded, eyes wide. "Much younger. Mid-thirties, max. Big hair. Tight jeans. Rhinestone-studded top. Linda says she looked like someone straight out of a 90s yearbook."

Cassandra frowned and sipped her tea. "A prom queen."

"Exactly what Linda said." Ruby leaned in. "What if he ran off with her?"

It was a deliciously scandalous possibility—and Cassandra hated that it made such perfect sense.

Later that afternoon, Cassandra slipped into the retreat's music room. Skye had locked herself in there earlier, strumming aimlessly on her guitar, her voice raspy with grief.

The room was empty now, but Cassandra could still feel the static of sadness in the air.

She scanned the space—half-empty wineglass on the piano, a silk scarf thrown across the armchair, and a notebook open on the music stand. Lyrics scrawled in rushed handwriting:

"He said forever, then disappeared / Left not a word, not even tears…"

Next to it, a half-written title: *The Widow Waltz.*

But it was the photo pinned under the glass paperweight that caught Cassandra's eye.

A faded yearbook picture, blown up and reprinted. A blonde woman beaming at the camera in a sequined dress, holding a tiara.

On the back: "To Troy, my forever dance partner. XO— C.J."

Cassandra turned it over again. The woman in the picture bore a striking resemblance to the mystery blonde Linda had described.

She didn't believe in coincidence.

"C.J.?" the barista said when Cassandra asked when she called into the Timberline Café. "Oh yeah. That's Charlene Jean McMillan. She moved back here a few months ago. Said she wanted to 'rekindle something.' Figured it was trouble the way she tossed her hair."

"And she was with Troy Landon?" Cassandra pressed.

"Sure was. Seemed cozy, if you ask me. He paid cash. Gave her his jacket on the way out."

Cassandra's suspicions crystallized like frost on a windowpane.

Troy had staged the whole thing. The moonlit paddle-board. The shoes. The sorrowful setup.

It was a vanishing act.

But the question still lingered like woodsmoke in the trees: Was it just an escape... or something more sinister?

CHAPTER FOUR

The next morning, Cassandra found Skye alone in the garden, barefoot on the frost-kissed grass, strumming her guitar with an eerie calm. Her signature red lipstick was smudged, her platinum curls in disarray. The melody was haunting—minor chords and sharp pauses like the pricking edge of a memory not fully grieved.

"He wrote me a promise in smoke and ash...
Then vanished like thunder, leaving only the flash..."

Not quite a lament.

Not quite a love song.

Definitely not a ballad of innocent heartbreak.

When Cassandra offered tea, Skye declined. "Only thing I need is revenge," she said with a smile too bitter to be staged. Then she laughed it off like she'd made a joke, but Cassandra didn't laugh with her.

Later that afternoon, Cassandra made her way to the guest suite Skye and Troy had shared. The bed was half-made. The windows were locked. But the room told a different story than the grieving widow had been selling.

In the wardrobe: a partially packed suitcase, neatly zipped with Troy's initials embossed in leather.

Tucked beneath it, a burned photo album, edges singed, the cover melted slightly as if someone had tried—and failed—to destroy it entirely.

Cassandra sat cross-legged on the rug and opened it carefully. The first page held a snapshot of Skye and Troy at a ski lodge, locked in a kiss beneath a banner that read "Second Chances Retreat – Love Reborn."

The next few pages had been torn out. Burnt edges curled inward like withered petals.

The only page left intact was a photo of Troy, younger, standing with a blonde woman who looked strikingly like the prom queen from the Timberline Café description.

Charlene Jean.

Skye had tried to burn the past. But something in her rage had stopped her from finishing the job.

Back in her studio, Cassandra replayed every moment since the disappearance.

The dramatic porch tears. The sudden songwriting frenzy. The bitter quips, the melodramatic toasts to lost love.

It wasn't adding up.

Had Skye helped Troy vanish, hoping for a glamorous new chapter they'd planned together?

Or had Troy played her, just like he may have played Charlene years ago?

And now that he was gone… was Skye planning to get even?

Cassandra looked again at the lyrics she'd scribbled down in her notebook:

"You promised me thunder,
But I bring the storm."

CHAPTER FIVE

The lake gave up its secret at dawn.

Cassandra was sipping her morning coffee on the wraparound porch when the sirens wailed—a mournful, rising note that cut through the birdsong and sent a shiver down her spine. Ruby came running, slippers half-on, her breath misting in the air.

"They've found a body," she said.

Cassandra was already moving.

Down by the reeds at the far end of the lake, Sheriff Tom Archer stood solemnly as deputies pulled the body from the water. It was tangled in cattails, sodden and still, face turned toward the sky.

At first glance, Cassandra expected Troy—his staged death finally revealed for what it was.

But as the face came into view, she drew a sharp breath. It wasn't Troy.

It was a woman.

Pale, blonde, her mascara still smudged beneath closed lids.

A rhinestone necklace caught the early light like frost on a spiderweb. One heel had come loose and dangled from a limp foot.

Charlene Jean.

The prom queen.

The woman Troy had allegedly run away with... was dead.

"She's been in the water at least a day," Tom said grimly. "No signs of an accident. Ligature marks. Defensive wounds. This was no drowning."

The news spread through Willow Hollow like spilled paint on canvas. The guests began whispering in corners, the media vans started circling like crows, and Skye?

Skye locked herself in the music room.

But not before Cassandra caught a glimpse of something red smeared across her wrist—lipstick, or blood, she couldn't be sure.

If Troy had vanished to be with Charlene, why was Charlene now dead?

Had Skye found them together?

Had Charlene discovered she was just another pawn?

Or had Troy planned this from the start—to disappear and leave both women behind... one grieving, one floating facedown in the lake?

The cozy retreat was now officially a crime scene.

And Cassandra knew this was no longer a story of heartbreak.

It was a story of betrayal, obsession... and murder.

CHAPTER SIX

Cassandra knew one thing for sure—Skye Newton wasn't the weeping widow she pretended to be.

She hadn't shed a tear for Charlene Jean. In fact, she hadn't emerged from her music room since the body was found—except once, to light a bonfire. Cassandra had seen the smoke curling over the pines at dawn, smelled the acrid burn of old paper and perfume.

She didn't wait for the sheriff to catch up. She knew instinctively: if she wanted the truth, she'd have to uncover it herself.

The investigation began with music.

Cassandra slipped into Skye's private studio after Skye left for town. The walls were lined with guitars, but it was the handwritten lyrics scattered on the piano that caught her eye.

She read them slowly, piecing them together like a melody from a broken tune.

"He took my heart and bled it dry,
Buried love beneath a lie.
But I kept the proof, I kept the song—
And I knew he wouldn't last long..."

A threat disguised as poetry.

In the bottom drawer, Cassandra found an envelope marked TROY—INSURANCE, filled with newspaper clippings, photos, and a typed note:

"If you leave me, this goes to TMZ."

There it was. Blackmail.

Skye hadn't just lost a husband—she'd once held him on a leash made of secrets.

Cassandra followed the trail back through old interviews, fan blogs, and obscure tabloid articles. She uncovered whispers of an affair Skye had with her former producer, and rumors of hush money paid to a session singer in Austin who'd claimed Troy fathered her child.

But it was a forgotten podcast interview that Cassandra discovered that made her pause.

"I've done things I'm not proud of," Troy's voice said, low and gravelly. "But everything I did, I did for love. I just wanted to be free."

Free from Skye?

Or from the mess he'd made with Charlene?

The final clue came from an unexpected place—Skye's backup singer, a young woman named Melody who had left the tour a year ago after "creative differences." Melody's Instagram told a story through art—painted lyrics of Skye's songs… and one chilling image: a man with Troy's face, puppet strings tied to his wrists, hanging from a lipstick-stained hand.

By nightfall, Cassandra sat with her journal open, pen in hand, the pieces swirling together like storm clouds over the lake.

Skye had motive. Skye had secrets. Skye had power.

But if Skye had killed Charlene Jean... where was Troy?

Why fake his own death, if not to escape both women?

Unless, of course... Troy never made it out of Willow Hollow either.

Cassandra closed her notebook.

She didn't have all the answers yet. But she could hear the chorus building.

Someone was orchestrating the whole thing.

And it was time to follow the next note.

CHAPTER SEVEN

I t started with a song.

Not one of Skye's chart-toppers, but a scratchy, warbled demo—recorded late at night on an old cassette and hidden behind a writing desk. Cassandra found it purely by accident, knocking over a vase while searching for more lyrics.

She pressed play.

"You always said she was nothing," a man's voice slurred. "Just a girl from high school. But you didn't see her face when I told her I was staying. She said she'd ruin everything."

Then a pause. The faint clink of ice in a glass.

"She grabbed the wheel. We were by the lake. I tried to stop her…"

Silence.

Then a low, exhausted whisper:

"But maybe it's better this way."

. . .

The next piece fell into place at the Willow Hollow café the next day, where Cassandra casually asked the waitress about the morning Troy disappeared.

"He was in here just after sunrise," the girl said, drying a mug. "Said he was heading to the cabin to think. Ordered a cinnamon roll. Seemed nervous."

"But Skye said he was paddleboarding."

The waitress shrugged. "Didn't look like a guy about to swim."

Skye's alibi had holes big enough to paddle a canoe through.

With the sheriff preoccupied organizing a search for "Troy's remains," Cassandra set off toward the northern end of the lake, where a crumbling trail led to an old artist's cabin long since forgotten.

The door creaked open with a push.

Inside: dust, old paintings... and a half-eaten cinnamon roll.

Then a muffled sound.

A thump.

Behind the curtain in the bedroom, Cassandra found Troy —alive, tied up, dazed but breathing.

"Skye," he whispered hoarsely. "She found me. She wanted me gone. But not like this..."

Cassandra returned to the retreat as the sun was setting— Skye was on stage rehearsing for a private benefit concert, bathed in golden light, strumming a mournful chord on her guitar.

"Funny thing about stories," Cassandra said from the back of the room, holding the tape recorder aloft. "They always find their chorus."

Skye's hands froze. Her eyes narrowed.

"You've been digging," she said.

"Charlene didn't ruin your marriage," Cassandra said quietly. "She ruined your control."

Skye rose from her stool, tall and dangerous in her snake-skin boots. "She was going to expose Troy. Make me a laughingstock. And he… he was going to let her."

"You staged his death to make him disappear. But Charlene wouldn't go quietly. So you made sure she never spoke again."

For a moment, Skye looked like she might deny it.

But then she smiled—cold, sad, and proud.

"No one writes my last verse," she said.

Sheriff Archer arrived moments later. Skye was arrested mid-song, her guitar still echoing through the valley.

Troy, shaken but safe, gave a full statement. Skye had lured Charlene to the lake under the pretense of reconciliation —and murdered her in a fit of jealous rage.

The puppet strings were cut.

But the echo of the music lingered.

CHAPTER EIGHT

W illow Hollow was quiet again.

The lake shimmered under the late summer sun, no longer hiding secrets beneath its glassy surface. The guests had returned to their workshops and nature walks. The whispers had dulled to murmurs. The shadow over the retreat had lifted—if only slightly.

Cassandra sat with a fresh pot of tea on the veranda, watching Matisse the cat chase a fluttering leaf across the boards. It had been a long week. A week of lies unraveled, of grief and greed masquerading as love, of music turned into motive.

Skye Newton was gone. She had been taken into custody quietly, without the press spectacle she once might have courted. A one-way flight back to Nashville awaited her, where a legal team and a long line of scandal-hungry journalists would pick apart the truth like vultures.

Her last song—left scrawled on a napkin in the lodge's lounge—read like a confession, or maybe a goodbye:

He said he'd stay, but hearts don't rhyme,
So I wrote the ending, line by line…

Even Troy, now free and quietly stunned, had said little since. He chose to leave Willow Hollow behind, hopping on a bus with nothing but a duffel bag and a battered cowboy hat. Cassandra doubted she'd ever see him again.

Ruby joined Cassandra on the porch, two steaming cups in hand.

"I can't believe it," she said softly. "She had everything. Fame. Fortune. Fans. Why throw it all away?"

"Because she couldn't control the story anymore," Cassandra replied. "And some people would rather destroy what they can't direct."

Ruby shook her head. "You always find the brushstrokes in the chaos."

Cassandra smiled. "That's what art teaches us—look deeper. There's always something hidden beneath the first layer."

As the sun slipped behind the mountains, casting shimmering light across the retreat, Cassandra felt something stir in her chest. A ripple in the peace. A knowing.

Because even though harmony had returned to Willow Hollow, it was the kind of harmony that the slightest discord could break. A secret too long buried. A stranger arriving on a stormy night. A painting that doesn't match the signature.

She'd been through enough mysteries to know one thing for certain:

Where there is beauty, fame, or fortune—

Trouble always finds its canvas.

COMING SOON

Four Cats, a Canvas, and a Corpse

At Willow Hollow, the cats may be curious—but it's Cassandra who uncovers the killer.

It's spring at Willow Hollow, and Cassandra is hosting a cat-themed art retreat for eccentric painters and their beloved felines. With four cats prowling the halls, a new guest with an attitude, and a priceless missing painting, Cassandra has her hands full.

But when one of the guests is found dead—face-down in a paint palette and surrounded by scratch marks—what started as a cozy gathering turns into a colorful case of murder by design.

As Cassandra untangles secrets hidden in sketches, catnip toys, and forged artworks, she'll need every brushstroke of intuition to solve a mystery that's anything but purr-fect.

Coming soon...

AUTHOR'S NOTE

When I first imagined Murder on the Lake, I envisioned a glamorous country music icon arriving in a tranquil small-town setting—radiant on the outside, but carrying the kind of secrets that ripple beneath even the stillest waters.

What I didn't expect was how close this story would mirror real life.

This book was loosely inspired by the strange and haunting true-life disappearance of Patrick McDermott, the former partner of Olivia Newton-John, who vanished during a fishing trip off the coast of California in 2005. Though many believed he had drowned, no body was ever found. Over the years, theories swirled—ranging from tragic accident to staged disappearance and beyond.

I was struck by how loss, love, and mystery can so easily intertwine—and how, for those left behind, not knowing can be more painful than the truth.

While Murder on the Lake is entirely fictional, it explores a similar emotional terrain: the grief that doesn't follow neat stages, the danger of perception over truth, and the hidden lives we carry behind our public selves. Like all cozy mysteries, it's also filled with wit, warmth, and (of course) a wise and whiskery cat.

I hope you enjoyed diving into this story as much as I loved writing it. And I hope, too, that it reminds you—like it reminded me—that even the deepest mysteries can one day surface.

With gratitude and curiosity,

Mollie Mathews

P.S. Enjoyed the mystery? Let others know!

If you loved *Murder on the Lake*, the best way to support this book—and help fellow cozy mystery lovers discover it— is by leaving a short review on Amazon or Goodreads.

Your thoughts don't need to be long or fancy. Just a sentence or two about what you enjoyed most. Reviews help this series grow and reach new readers—and it means the world to me.

Thank you for being part of Cassandra Fairweather's sleuthing journey!

Read on for an excerpt from *Murder on the Canvas* and *The Italian Billionaire's Scandalous Marriage*, book two in the Gemstone Billionaires series. A wonderful mystery where a painting holds many secrets. Each story can be read as a stand-alone novel.

If you'd like to learn more about these characters, gain inside tips into the writing process, or be the first to know when a new book is released, subscribe to my newsletter here: http://eepurl.com/ghM501

Please email me and I'll be in touch personally—I promise…mollie@molliemathews.com.

EXCERPT: MURDER ON THE CANVAS

Cassandra Fairweather adjusted the brim of her sunhat as she surveyed the grounds of the Willow Hollow Art Retreat. The Montana sun cast a warm golden glow over the meadow, painting the landscape in hues that would inspire even the most jaded of artists. A gentle breeze rustled through the towering pines, carrying with it the scent of wildflowers and fresh earth. It was the perfect day to welcome her new group of artists—and potential murderers, as her sense of intuition whispered.

"Stop it," she muttered to herself, brushing a wisp of silver-streaked hair from her forehead. "Not every event ends in disaster."

The annual Plein Air Painting Competition was her pride and joy, a weeklong escape for artists seeking inspiration in nature's splendor. This year's guest list was an eclectic mix of talent, ambition, and ego—a combination Cassandra knew could be combustible. She straightened her blouse, readying herself for the first round of introductions.

The crunch of gravel under tires drew her attention to the

retreat's driveway. A sleek black car rolled to a stop, and out stepped Victor Deveraux, the event's celebrity judge. Even from a distance, Victor's presence was as sharp as the tailored lines of his suit. His salt-and-pepper hair was meticulously combed, his expression one of faint amusement—like a man who already knew he was the smartest person in the room.

"Cassandra," he said, his voice smooth as silk as he extended a hand. "Always a pleasure to return to your charming little retreat."

"Victor," Cassandra replied, clasping his hand briefly. "I see you haven't lost your flair for dramatics."

He chuckled, but his eyes swept the grounds with a calculating gaze. "Charm and simplicity. You do know how to set a scene. Let's hope the contestants live up to it."

Cassandra bit back a retort as Victor strode toward the main lodge. She'd dealt with his ego before, but it seemed sharper this year, more biting. As she watched him go, another car arrived, this one a battered sedan that creaked in protest as its driver stepped out.

"Lila Patterson," Cassandra called out, smiling warmly.

The young artist grinned back, her oversized canvas bag swinging from one shoulder. "Cassandra! This place is even more beautiful than I imagined. I've been counting the days to get here."

Cassandra took in Lila's eager expression, her freckled face already glowing with excitement. "I'm glad you're here. We've got quite the group this year."

Lila glanced toward Victor's retreating figure. "And him?"

"Victor Deveraux," Cassandra said, lowering her voice. "He's judging the competition."

Lila's smile faltered, replaced by something more guarded. "I've heard of him. Didn't he…?"

"Let's just say Victor has a way of making an impression," Cassandra interrupted, steering the conversation back to lighter topics. "Why don't you get settled in? Your cabin is the second one on the left."

One by one, the remaining participants arrived, each bringing their own energy to the retreat. There was **Greg Thornton**, the boisterous sponsor of the event, who wasted no time boasting about his company's top-tier art supplies. **Sophia Knight**, Victor's nervous assistant, carried herself like a shadow, slipping unnoticed into the background. **David Granger**, a retired lawyer, greeted Cassandra with a firm handshake and a twinkle of mischief in his eye. By the time everyone was settled, Cassandra's instincts were already on edge.

That evening, the group gathered for the welcome dinner on the lodge's veranda. Candlelight flickered over plates of roast chicken and herb-crusted potatoes as Cassandra raised her glass for a toast.

"To creativity, camaraderie, and the beauty of nature," she said, her voice carrying over the hum of conversation. "May this week inspire your best work yet."

The toast was met with murmurs of agreement and the clinking of glasses, but the convivial atmosphere didn't last. Victor, as was his style, made sure of that.

"While we're on the subject of inspiration," he said, setting down his fork with a theatrical flourish, "let me remind you all that beauty isn't enough. True art demands vision, technique, and—most importantly—courage."

His gaze landed on Lila, who stiffened under the scrutiny. "Do you have courage, Miss Patterson?" he asked.

Lila's cheeks flushed as she met his stare. "I think my work speaks for itself."

Victor smirked. "Does it? We'll see."

Greg Thornton cleared his throat, clearly uncomfortable. "Come now, Victor, we're here to support these artists, not tear them down."

Victor turned his attention to Greg, his smirk widening. "Ah, yes, Greg Thornton. Always the patron, never the artist. Tell me, does your generosity come with a price?"

Cassandra stepped in, her voice sharp. "Victor, perhaps you'd like to save your critiques for the judging panel."

"Of course," Victor said, raising his glass in mock contrition. "Far be it from me to ruin the mood."

The table fell into an uneasy silence, the clinking of utensils the only sound as the meal continued. Cassandra's gaze lingered on each of the guests, noting their reactions: Lila's simmering anger, Greg's visible discomfort, Sophia's darting eyes, and David's cold, calculating expression.

As the evening wound down, Cassandra stood on the lodge's porch, watching the stars emerge over the mountains. The peacefulness of the scene felt at odds with the tension brewing among her guests.

"Not every event ends in disaster," she reminded herself again. But the memory of Victor's smirk—and the looks it had drawn—made her stomach tighten with unease.

Little did she know, the first stroke of tragedy had already been painted.

* * *

Did you enjoy reading this excerpt?
Book One in the Montana Cozy Art Mystery series available
now

EXCERPT: THE ITALIAN BILLIONAIRE'S SCANDALOUS MARRIAGE

THE ITALIAN BILLIONAIRE'S SCANDALOUS MARRIAGE

Mollie Mathews

Blue Orchid Publishing

PROLOGUE

'You should never have responded to that email. I don't understand you, Alexandra.' Bitterness bled from her mother's words.

Alex Spencer pressed her lips together, momentarily fixing her gaze on the desolate New York sky as snow began to fall. 'Okay, so an email arrives out of the blue telling me the man who I thought was my father *isn't*,' she said, shoveling summer clothes into a well-traveled leopard-print suitcase. 'And then I find out my real father is dead and he's left me some valuable paintings—and I'm supposed to ignore that?'

'Why do you insist on digging up the past? I've told you no good will come of it.'

Alex knew they would never agree. She wanted to say, "Mom, why are you making everything so difficult? Why won't you talk to me about my father? Why didn't you tell me the truth?" But she'd already tried, and every time her mother evaded answering. Despite what her mother had done, for the sake of their tie of blood, which was the only thing left between them, she had to keep the peace.

'Why do you have to go back to New Zealand? What more do you hope to achieve that wasn't settled six months ago? What point is there?' Elizabeth Spencer pressed, fixing disapproving eyes on her errant daughter.

'You know why I need to go back, Mother,' Alex said quietly, careful to stop exasperation creeping into her voice.

Her mother's brown eyes turned a chilly shade of black. 'After all Charles and I have done for you,' she spat. 'He's been more of a father to you than that man ever was.' Although she would never say it, the accusation whistled through her mother's pursed lips. *Why would you want to do something so selfish?*

Alex forced herself to count to ten. It was as if her mother thought keeping something so important a secret from her own daughter all these years was no big deal. It was as though she thought that replacing a real dad with a surrogate dad gave her a stable identity.

How could Alex possibly explain without severing their relationship for good? Finally, she knew why she had never felt understood, never felt accepted, never felt she belonged. And while everything was such a mystery she knew that she could never find peace until she understood her past.

'Mom, I told you when I came back for Christmas that I'd only be here for a few weeks. Please don't let us spend our last moments arguing.' Alex forced an uncertain smile hoping it would melt her mother's iciness.

Her boutique travel business meant she was never home for long. She was like those dandelions; settling for a spell then drifting away. She was no longer a child. Yet in this matter she longed for her mother's approval.

'Why can't you let go of this thing you've got about your father?' Her mother fired. 'What more do you have to know,

for heaven's sake? He was an artist. He left you a few paintings. End of story.'

It wasn't the end of the story. Far from it. In fact of the six
paintings her biological father had left her in his will she
knew with gut-churning clarity that only one would unlock
buried secrets. Secrets her mother seemed resolute never to
divulge

'I want to know everything. I want to know about the man
whose blood courses through my veins. I want to know who I
am. Why can't you understand that?'

'There's nothing more to say. I was young. Impulsive. He
was a mistake.'

Alex's stomach clenched. *She was a mistake.* Her mother
didn't have to say it but her tone made it clear.

She was the girl nobody wanted.

CHAPTER ONE

A lex pressed against a pillar beneath the cavernous ceiling of the Auckland art gallery, suppressing a yawn as she fought a wave of jet lag. Clutching the exhibition catalog to her chest she swept her gaze over the crowd gathered for the opening of the dazzling retrospective exhibition of her father's lifeworks. Only yesterday she had been in icy New York and now here she was in the heat of the New Zealand summer, surrounded by Veuve Clicquot, popping corks and intoxicating works of art.

At the center of the gallery stood Clive Gacos, the art dealer who had discovered the man she now knew was her father, exchanging air kisses and handshakes. Impeccably armored in a steel-grey designer suit that complemented his trademark helmet of silver hair he looked in his element as he enthusiastically greeted a procession of art collectors and socialites.

Alex crossed her arms protectively over her chest as women flashed him far too-enthusiastic smiles, and fluttered acrylic nails in shallow waves. She hated crowds at the best of times and tonight, surrounded by so much pretense, she felt doubly out of her comfort zone. Nausea crawled through her stomach as she wondered if Clive's insistence that she exhibit the painting had been one giant mistake.

Would tonight flush out someone intimately connected to the powerful, yet haunting image? Someone who would help her unearth the past her mother and step-father were so determined to keep buried?

Her gaze drifted to the vast landscape her father had painted running the length of the far wall. Lost Love. Two words that tore her heart apart. Looking at the painting now she wondered if the name she'd given it still fitted. For some inexplicable reason, unlike all her father's other artworks, he'd left this one unnamed. Why did he leave so few clues to its meaning?

Barely conscious of the crowd pressing around her Alex's heart quickened as she scanned the craggy Southern Ranges, their soaring peaks troughed on the canvas with a hurtle of blue and ochre and gold. Her gaze honed in on the hauntingly beautiful face of a woman, infused within the rocks. Why had her father painted a woman's face into the landscape? And whose was it—so beautiful?

The woman seemed to reach through time and space, lifting agonized eyes, calling Alex's name, drawing her deeper and deeper into the painting's mystery. Instinct told her something deeply personal had happened to inspire the painting, something that could shed light on her past? For twenty-five years her life had been a lie. Months of searching for clues to her past had ended in granite walls of silence.

Yet the way her heart pounded, her eyes pooled with tears, and every hair on her body stood on end each time she looked at the painting, told her that there was a deeper reason her father wanted the painting to remain in her possession. Alex was sure her father was enticing her to discover the painting's secrets. Why else did he leave this particular painting in his will to the daughter he'd never met?

She tore herself away from Lost Love and stood at a distance observing people's reactions in the hope that she would discover someone who found the painting as meaningful as she did. An older woman stared at it the longest, her eyes pooling as she fingered the elaborate gold locket at her throat.

A young man and woman holding hands stopped in front of it, and the woman slipped her palm from her partner's as she stepped closer to study the face of the woman. A middle-aged man's body grew hard and tense as he looked, and he passed quickly by. Another man with a receding hairline flinched as if someone had punched him in the gut. He reached a hand out to the painting, not quite touching the velvet plains of golden tussock and Rātā trees clinging fiercely to craggy rocks.

Dread wormed through her. The strange and enigmatic image evoked powerful reactions in them all, but none of them betrayed the fact they held the missing piece to her painful puzzle. She pressed her lips together, holding her face tight, as tears pricked her eyes. Showing Lost Love was a hair-brained idea, like searching for a needle in a field of grass. What real chance did she have of discovering someone who knew anything truly intimate about her dead father? Yet what else could she do? All her other inquiries had come to nothing.

Alex heaved a sigh of frustration and turned away. From across the gallery, Clive Gacos caught her anxious gaze. His fluttering fingers flourished a greeting across the room as he slithered to her side. 'Lost Love. I still think the title's morbid.'

He cocked his head to one side as his gaze darted from

the catalog to the painting before resting on Alex. 'Couldn't you have come up with something more commercial?'

Alex wanted to cry out, "It's how I feel." Instead, she said, 'You may be right, Mr. Gacos,' painting a mask of detached aloofness on her face. Instinct told her Clive was only interested in his fame and glory—not her own painful story. She took his outstretched hand and felt a shiver snake through her spine as cold, steely fingers shook hers.

'It's a fabulous turnout, my dear.' Bleached white teeth flashed a self-satisfied smile. "I'm absolutely delighted.'

'Are you sure that this is the best way to unearth someone who may know something about this painting, Mr. Gacos? You know how firmly my father was against it being exhibited.'

'Field of Dreams or Secret Passion would have been better. The right title can really boost sales,' he said glancing at the painting.

'That's interesting', Alex said flatly. 'But Lost Love is not for sale.'

Eerie, pale eyes looked right through her. 'My dear, everything is for sale.'

'No, Mr. Gacos. It's not. I'm looking for answers. A sale won't achieve that.' Had she been wrong to trust him? Was he just another person in a long line of people to deceive her? 'Besides you told me yourself, my father made it quite clear that the painting must never leave my possession.'

'My dear, 40 years in the industry has taught me one thing, what an artist says and what an artist means are quite different things. If you gave me ten dollars for every time I've heard, "This is my favorite work, I'll never part with it," or some other nonsense, I'd be a hundred-fold richer.' His reptilian eyes scanned her face as though searching for a weakness in her resolve. 'Of course, none of this matters now that your father is dead.'

Dead.

Alex's eyes misted as the finality of the word hit her. It was ridiculous. Eleven months ago she hadn't even known geologist, turned painter, Ted Carr, known in art circles as Jimmie Goldie, was her father and since then she'd had plenty of time to accept the fact that he was gone. But she couldn't help feeling regret.

If only she'd known her father. If only he was by her side now. Although in a strange way he was, she mused, her eyes misting as she gazed at the painting. Infused with his energy, his passion, his spirit, Lost Love was her only link. It was as though the painting was his voice—allowing him to speak through time and space. But only to those with eyes that could see and ears that could hear, and Alex still had no idea what he was saying.

Maybe she was reading too much into it. Maybe it was just a painting. But why did her father demand it never be exhibited in public? And why did he want her to have it?

'I expect this exhibition to arouse even more interest in Jimmie's work, and the longer we hold off the more the painting will appreciate in value,' Clive blabbered on, oblivious of her raw grief.

Alex clenched her teeth, shutting back a retort at his thoughtless remark. This wasn't the time to be emotional, nor to incite conflict. She hated disharmony and discord. And although she'd been continually teased because she always chose the peaceful route, putting him in his place would only get him offside.

'Remind me again Mr. Gacos, just how well did you know my father?' she said gently.

'I told you—I discovered him. Made him a sell-out success.'

'Yes, but what was he really like?'

'I don't know. We never met.'

'But you were his dealer?'

'I deal in works of art, Miss Spencer. Not people. Besides, your father liked his privacy. I respected that.'

'Didn't you wonder why he hid his true identity?'

'My dear, half the celebrities in the world use fake, made-up names. Careers live and die by people's memorability. It's all part of the game. Do you really think Andy Warhol's paintings would sell for astronomical sums if he went by his real name, Andrew Warhola? Your father was smart. Jimmie Goldie, or Ted Carr—ask yourself, who's the better investment?'

Tension knotted her shoulders. She was getting nowhere.

'Want some advice?'

No.

'Take it from me. There's no mystery—just a finely executed brand strategy. And you are the lucky beneficiary. So what? He left you this painting. Maybe his conscience got the better of him. In my opinion, it's an exceptional piece of work, one of his finest, and tantalizingly one that the art world has never seen before. If I were you, I'd sell it. Realize the cash. Return to New York. Go live your life.'

Go live your life. She would—but not before she had her answers. Alex's gaze drifted back to the crowd. Her only hope was that someone would reveal something in their reaction to the painting. Surely if anyone was connected intimately it would hit them with the same power-punch to the gut as it did to her every time she looked at it.

Suddenly she was distracted by a blaze of rustic color as

the most ridiculously handsome man Alex had ever seen strode toward her.

CHAPTER TWO

His six-foot frame wore an immaculately tailored camel jacket, cut from the finest Merino wool and fashionably faded jeans gracing a powerful physique.

His skin was deeply tanned, his hair rich dark chocolate with golden highlights—wavy and slightly tousled. Not a classically handsome pasty metro-sexual like the American suitors her mother continually threw in her path. But a ruggedly handsome man, who looked as though he would be equally at home in a New York boardroom dressed in a sleek Armani suit as he would be rustling cattle in a tough New Zealand Swandri. The man oozed passion, purpose—and danger.

She watched entranced as his gaze swept the room, standing rigidly in the archway with a presence that emanated command. He had a strong, arresting face, coldly handsome with no lines of weakness. A disturbingly primitive tug of attraction quaked through her body. She could imagine this man commanding a Roman Legion, or leading a charge of Templar Knights.

He oozed the power of a leader who made his own rules, ruthlessly sweeping aside anyone who stood in opposition. A smile fluttered to her lips as she imagined the shock on her mother's face if she married a man so raw and rugged. To her discomfort, she found the idea thrilling and quickly sanctioned her recklessness.

Whether the Adonis had read her mind Alex had no idea, but as he carved his way through the crowded gallery he slowed his stride. He paused opposite her and looked at her, a flicker of recognition glancing across his face as though he wondered if he had met her before, perhaps even bedded her.

His gaze narrowed with the level unwavering gaze of a ravenous lion. Whatever he was thinking Alex's heart raced. It was as if he could see right through to the essence of who she really was. It was as thrilling as it was intoxicating and disturbing. Near them people glided around the paintings, the vacuous height of the vaulted gallery ceiling amplifying people's voices, but she was trapped with him in exploding silence.

Usually, she dismissed such attention. But this was more than a fleeting appraisal of desirability, more than an appreciation of the curvaceous femininity of her figure. It was an arrogant assessment projecting the confident knowledge that he could have her if he wanted. The only question appeared to be could he be bothered?

A frisson of danger scuttled down Alex's spine. Under his penetrating gaze, she felt like a naked model posing for a ravenous sculptor. She picked at the black sequins of her dress, immediately regretting wearing the figure-hugging cocktail number she'd purchased for the formal opening night.

She never wore dresses ordinarily and hated wearing black, but she had wanted to blend in with the art-gallery-noir that she knew everyone else would be wearing. It was the only suitable dress she'd found at the second-hand store on Queen Street in the few hours she had to spare since arriving in Auckland. As her face flared with humiliating heat Alex tugged the bottom of the clinging dress, cursing the shimmering sequins and the above-knee length for attracting his attention.

His piercing green eyes rested for long, uneasy moments on Alex's quivering lips. The perfect lushness of his mouth quirked dangerously as his gaze inched with leisurely thoroughness before dropping to where her dress clung to her chest.

Every whisper of hair on her body stood like sentries armed for defense. Yet to her intense humiliation she found her barriers weakened. Was it pleasure? Longing? Or desire she felt flood her body with warmth? She couldn't be sure. It had been years since she'd been with a man, and never with anyone certainly so virile. For the briefest moment, she found herself wondering what it would be like to be taken by him. Every remnant of her rational mind fought the dangerous feeling, but the more she struggled the more her body betrayed her.

Suddenly, with an air of explosive tension, the weight of the stranger lurched forward. His face spun away from her. Alex followed the direction of his fixed gaze, piqued that his interest in her had been so totally diverted. She couldn't see his expression but she could sense his undiluted fury.

In the next instant, he propelled himself through the crowd, a dozen lithe strides bringing him within a foot of *Lost Love*.

Her pulse rate ricocheted as she watched transfixed as the stranger froze as if in shock, then shook his head in disbelief. After several tense moments, he rifled through the catalog he carried. His shoulders tensed as he read the small caption, then scrutinized the painting again. He thrust his arms out as if to wrench it from the wall. His hand tightened into a closed fist crumpling the catalog, then thrust it into his pocket.

Alex's heart pounded then took a dive. Her mind raced ahead as she struggled to understand the intensity of his reaction. Could he unravel her mysterious past?

He swung around, his face set in determined purpose, his gaze scanning quickly over the people in the room. They passed over Alex without a flicker of recognition, every muscle of his face taunt with savagery.

'Who is he?'

'I don't know, but he looks important—and *very* wealthy.' Clive said in a low voice. 'Let me handle this.'

Clive was off and moving with the silent speed of a cobra toward the stranger before Alex could object. Tension jack-knifed through her chest. What should she do? Run after Clive and risk getting in the way? The stranger had dismissed any interest in her with the aloof detachment of a man who would never cede control. Instinct told Alex where she was concerned he was untamable. Like a wild wolf, the wrong move would send him running. Besides, Clive's reputation for netting the elusive was legendary.

She reached for a glass of champagne from a passing waitress and took tiny gulps as she hovered anxiously. Would Clive find out what had incited such a powerful reaction? Would the stranger reveal why he had responded so strongly?

Perhaps the painting incited something deep within his soul, she wondered. No that was impossible. The brute didn't appear to have a soul or he wouldn't have dismissed her so coolly. Her heart pulsed with the sting of his rejection. He was clearly a collector like many others in the gallery. A numbers man who no doubt prided himself on his many conquests and the number of artworks he possessed.

Alex gripped the stem of the glass as she watched the scene unfold. As Clive tried to beguile him with his charming smile the stranger's shoulders tensed. Fear rumbled through her as cataclysmic as an earthquake. Was Clive failing? She cursed herself for allowing him to take the lead. A woman with a beehive hairdo, her long neck over-saturated with Opium perfume paused in front of her obstructing her view.

'Excuse me,' Alex said, inhaling a heady mix of cinnamon and spice, as she pressed past the woman. The stranger was no longer in front of the painting. Her heart hammered as she stood on her tiptoes and scoured the room. Where had he gone?

A slice of golden caramel moving like a bullet caught her eye as the stranger strode toward the exit. Then, like the sun setting over the ranges in *Lost Love* in a blink he was gone.

CHAPTER THREE

Despite the fatigue that had seeped into every bone in her body, Alex was still awake, her mind whirring with a kaleidoscope of possible scenarios, when the telephone in her hotel room rang. 'Who could that be?'

She glanced at the digital clock on the bedside table. Ten thirty-five pm. In New York it would be Saturday and her mother and Charles would have just finished a leisurely brunch. Alex propped herself on her pillows and lifted the telephone receiver, bracing herself for the inquisition.

But it wasn't an international call.

'Sorry if I've disturbed you, Alexandra,' Clive Gacos rattled over the line, 'I know it's late but I couldn't wait,' he pressed on, sounding not in the least bit sorry. 'I've received an offer for one of your father's paintings. I've been instructed to close the deal tonight.' He paused, then continued, his tone pinched, 'If you're agreeable, of course.'

An odd feeling of premonition crawled through Alex's chest. 'Which painting, Mr Gacos?'

Clive hesitated then cleared his throat. '*Lost Love*. I've been negotiating on your behalf throughout the evening.'

Her shoulder's tensed. 'Negotiating what on my behalf?'

'You won't believe it. I can hardly believe it myself. It's the stuff of dreams,' he gasped, nearly tripping over his excitement. 'Before you say anything, the client has been informed, as per your instructions, that *Lost Love* is not for sale.' Clive rushed on, obviously anxious to defer her refusal. 'However, the offer he is making...it's simply staggering. I didn't feel I could say no. Not without consulting you of course, my dear.'

'You know I can't sell.' Alex said annoyed at the patronizing attitude that snaked through his voice.

'I know. I know,' he repeated, in barely held exasperation. 'But Alex, it wasn't written in his will. There's nothing legally binding.'

'My father was adamant that the painting remain in my possession.'

Clive took a deep breath. 'Alexandra, I don't think you realize how much money is at stake. This is big—'

'No figure would be large enough to make me betray my father's trust, Mr Gacos.' Her throat felt like sandpaper and she reached for the glass of Pellegrino on the bedside table.

'Five million dollars!' he blurted. 'Think how that would change your life.'

The glass slid from her hand. Alex pushed back the blankets and jumped to her feet, her mind spinning. 'What did you say?' Alex kept her voice calm, but the rush pounded through her now, the painting, the adrenaline, five million dollars.

'Five...million...dollars! I think even your father would agree. None of us could have predicted such a meteoric rise in prices for his work. Selling now would catapult your father's name into artistic infamy. Just think what you would be doing for his reputation. 'It's a record sum for a New Zealand artist. Quite dazzling. But we must move quickly.'

What was the urgency? Clive's pressure addled her brain. Was notoriety what her father wanted? It took a few more stunned moments before she managed to speak again. 'Is this for real?'

'I can assure you the buyer is quite serious.' Clive replied infusing his voice with professional stoicism, but she sensed the zealous excitement he was suppressing. The commission on five million dollars was obviously blinding.

She could well imagine how brokering a deal of this size would clinch Clive's well known ambition to join the elite club of the world's most powerful art dealers. Had the painting been for sale she may have admired his ambitious drive, perhaps even been grateful, but it wasn't for sale, and he was clearly driven by his own self-interest. But what Clive wanted was none of her concern. For once what she wanted would be her dominant priority.

Recovering from the initial shock Alex's mind kicked up a gear. Someone wanted that painting very badly. The question was, who and why?

'Who is the buyer?' she asked, keeping her tone even.

'They have asked to remain anonymous.'

'Of course they have,' she said, wearily.

'I honestly don't know. In this type of situation, the bids always come through a third party. Some people don't wish to be in the spotlight. However, I can assure you the offer is authentic. Just say "yes" and the money will be in your bank account tomorrow.'

Someone wanted the painting desperately. This was what she had hoped for, it was the sole reason she'd agreed the painting be put on exhibition—and the response was beyond her wildest dreams. She had to figure this out carefully. If she couldn't get through all the middlemen she'd blow the opportunity to find out if the person behind the offer knew anything of her father's past.

Alex paced the room, her tension growing. When at last she spoke it was in a flat, detached voice.

'Mr Gacos, tell the intermediaries that unless I deal with the buyer directly there is absolutely no chance of a deal.'

'It's not the done thing,' he spluttered.

'Then I guess it's goodnight,' she bluffed, hoping he didn't detect the squeak in her voice.

'Wait. I'll pass on your instructions. Hold the line.'

Alex's hands trembled as she pressed the cordless phone to her ear and paced the room, her tension growing as the minutes ticked by. She felt desperately tired, but her mind was spinning. Her demand must be meeting with resistance. A great deal of resistance. Hopefully that was a good sign.

'I'm sorry. The buyer is not prepared to discuss the matter in person. It's your decision but I firmly believe if you refuse their terms the bidder will disappear.'

Alex's head pulsed. She had nothing to go on. But if someone was prepared to offer that much, she didn't believe they would walk away. They had to be bluffing to force a quick decision. Bad luck for them that they had seriously underestimated her motivation. No amount of money would ever persuade her to give up *Lost Love*. And now that she knew someone else wanted to possess the painting as badly as she wanted to keep it she was even more determined to follow the trail. She knew now, without a doubt, that *Lost Love* held some special significance to someone else. She took a long, deep breath, needing to slow her pulse-rate before she threw down her last card.

'The answer is no,' she said flatly. 'You can tell them I will never sell to a stranger. They know how to reach me if they change their mind.'

'Alexandra—' She could hear the hiss of Clive's breath as he bit back a protest. 'Very well. As you wish. I'll pass on your reply.' His tone held a note of desperation.

Alex sat on the bed, slid back on the pillows and tried to relax. It was utterly impossible. Her mind kept racing backwards and forwards. Had she played the right hand? She couldn't think how she could have played it differently. Until the buyer made his decision she couldn't plan her next move. But that didn't stop her volleying the possibilities around in her mind.

It was a longer wait this time, but Alex didn't mind. Each minute that passed increased her hope. Obviously they were talking very seriously, and she had no doubt that Clive's tenacity would keep the deal alive.

'Alex—' The note of relief in Clive's voice brought an elated smile to her lips. 'The principal insists that the meeting be kept completely confidential.'

'Absolutely,' she agreed quickly.

'And it has to be tomorrow morning. As early as you can make it.'

The buyer was clearly impatient. While Alex needed as much time with the mysterious person as possible, she just wasn't a morning girl. And since she held the trump card at the moment she would call the shots.

'Lunch near my hotel would suit me better.' She glanced out the window at the Sky Tower dominating the skyline with its commanding presence. 'The Orbit Revolving Restaurant,' she said impulsively. 'Eleven-thirty.'

There was only a short pause before Clive came back with the reply. 'Agreed.'

'How will I recognize them? Don't tell me—red carnation, dark glasses?' she said flippantly.

'I'll be there, Alexandra,' he said quickly. 'To introduce you and to represent your interests.'

'No, Clive. I'm sorry.'

He heaved a reluctant sigh. 'Of course.' A pregnant pause crackled down the line. 'Will you sell, Alexandra?'

'Thank you for negotiating the meeting, Mr Gacos.' She forced her voice to a nonchalant crawl. 'Good night, Mr Gacos. I'll let you know the outcome.'

A Tsunami of exhaustion, anxiety, apprehension and excitement crawled over her as she put the phone down. Maybe the buyer just loved the painting. But it didn't stack up. Five million dollars spelled out a compulsive desire to acquire, and there had to be some reason for it over and above the usual obsession of an art-lover. Her father, while popular in New Zealand, was no Da Vinci. It could hardly be an investment buy at that price. So that left—what?

She stared out the window at the fiery red neon lights of the Sky Tower. Meeting so close to Auckland's casino seemed ironically appropriate. Everything about the meeting was a gamble and she would need to play a skillful hand if she were to win. Would lady luck be her ally or would she shine her benevolent light on the mysterious, but clearly determined opponent?

* * *

Did you enjoy reading this excerpt?
Book One in the Gemstone Billionaires series **available now**

ABOUT THE AUTHOR

MOLLIE MATHEWS is an award-winning artist and author. With a passion for creativity and a keen eye for detail, she crafts enchanting cozy mysteries that blend her love of art, small-town charm, and the irresistible pull of a good whodunit.

Drawing inspiration from her own experiences as an artist and her fascination with the secrets hidden in everyday life, Mollie brings her stories to life with vibrant characters, intriguing twists, and picturesque settings that transport readers to another world.

Why Cozy Art Mysteries?

Mollie has always believed that art is more than just beauty on a canvas—it's a window into human emotions, relationships, and, sometimes, hidden truths. In her **Montana Cozy Art Mysteries**, she captures the magic of art retreats, the camaraderie of small-town life, and the thrill of solving mysteries.

Set against the breathtaking Montana mountains, her series invites readers to Willow Hollow, a haven for artists where inspiration flourishes—but so do secrets and intrigue.

Her protagonist, Cassandra Fairweather, embodies Mollie's passion for art and curiosity for life's hidden layers. With a blend of wit, warmth, and determination, Cassandra guides readers through mysteries that are as heartwarming as they are suspenseful.

When Mollie's Not Writing...

When she's not weaving mysteries, Mollie can often be found painting in her studio, walking through nature for inspiration, or curled up with a cup of tea and a good book. Her favorite moments include visiting art galleries, exploring small towns, and dreaming up her next story.

Connect with Mollie Mathews:

Mollie loves hearing from her readers! Whether you want to share your thoughts on her books, discuss art and creativity, or simply say hello, you can connect with her through:

• **Website:** www.molliemathews.com

• **Newsletter:** Sign up for updates on new releases and exclusive content: http://eepurl.com/ghM501

• **Social Media:** Follow her on:

Facebook—https://www.facebook.com/molliemathewsnz

Instagram—https://www.instagram.com/molliemathewsauthor

for behind-the-scenes peeks at her writing and art.

Discover the magic of art, the charm of small-town life, and the thrill of a good mystery with Mollie Mathews and her Montana Cozy Art Mysteries.

BY MOLLIE MATHEWS

THE SHEIKHS UNTAMED BRIDES

CLAIMED BY THE SHEIKH
STOLEN BY THE SHEIKH
BOUGHT BY THE SHEIKH
FORGOTTEN BY THE SHEIKH
UNTAMED BY THE SHEIKH
UNVEILED BY THE SHEIKH
DECEIVED BY THE SHEIKH
THE SHEIKHS UNTAMED BRIDES BOX SET BOOKS 1-2
THE SHEIKHS UNTAMED BRIDES BOX SET BOOKS 1-3
THE SHEIKHS UNTAMED BRIDES BOX SET BOOKS 1-5

GEMSTONE BILLIONAIRES

THE ITALIAN BILLIONAIRE'S CHRISTMAS BRIDE

THE ITALIAN BILLIONAIRE'S SCANDALOUS MARRIAGE
THE ITALIAN BILLIONAIRE'S SAPPHIRE BRIDE
THE ITALIAN BILLIONAIRE'S LEGACY OF LOVE
GEMSTONE BILLIONAIRES 2 BOOK-BUNDLE BOX SET
GEMSTONE BILLIONAIRES 3 BOOK-BUNDLE BOX SET

TRUE LOVE

LOVE IN VENICE (3rd place winner Koru Award)
LOVE IN MEXICO
LOVE IN SICILY
LOVE IN MONTANA
LOVE IN TUSCANY
LOVE IN GREECE
LOVE IN SANTORINI

MONTANA HEARTS
A CHRISTMAS OF HER OWN
EVERLASTING CHRISTMAS

MONTANA COZY ART MYSTERIES
MURDER ON THE CANVAS
MURDER IN THE FRAME
MURDER IN THE PALETTE
MURDER ON THE LAKE
MONTANA COZY ART MYSTERIES 2 BOOK-BUNDLE BOX SET

NASHVILLE HEARTS

ONE STEP AT A TIME
LOVE RISING

PASSION DOWN UNDER SASSY SHORT STORIES

TWIST OF FATE
LOVE ME FOREVER
FOREVER AND ALWAYS
LOVE ME AS I AM
THE LIGHTKEEPER'S LOVER
FINDING A HUSBAND
LOVE ALL OF ME
CRAZY FOR YOU

PASSION DOWN UNDER 2 BOOK-BUNDLE BOX SET
(Books 1 & 2)
PASSION DOWN UNDER 3 BOOK-BUNDLE BOX SET
(Books 1, 2 & 3)
PASSION DOWN UNDER 6 BOOK-BUNDLE BOX SET

SHORT, SWEET SHEIKH LOVE STORIES
DESTINY
LUCKY

BITTERSWEET LOVE STORIES
WHAT IS SOFT IS STRONG

NASHVILLE HEARTS

ONE STEP AT A TIME
LOVE RISING

FLOURISHING HEARTS
THE GIRL IN PINK SKATES

ISBN eBook

ISBN print: 978-1-991374-16-5

Published by

Blue Orchid Publishing New Zealand

Blue Orchid
PUBLISHING

Visit www.molliemathews.com to read more about all our books and to buy them. You will also find features, author interviews and news of author events, and you can sign up for e-newsletters so that you're always first to hear about our new releases.